M. A. Ferguson

Special Thanks

To the GG Group for your invaluable support
and encouragement.

✦ Chapter 1 : The Arrival ✦

The autumn air was crisp as our moving van rolled into Salem, Massachusetts. Vibrant hues of red, orange, and gold adorned the trees lining the streets, casting a  warm glow on the historic buildings.

I peered out the window with a mix of excitement and apprehension. I had never lived in such an old-fashioned town before, and the thought of starting at a new school made my stomach flutter.

"Here we are, folks," Dad exclaimed, gesturing towards the two-story Victorian house with a wide grin.

"Our new home sweet home!" My younger brother, Alex, bounced out of the van with boundless energy, eager to explore our new surroundings. But I remained rooted to my seat, a sense of unease settling over me. Mom turned to me with a warm smile, her eyes full of understanding.

"It's going to be okay, Addison. Change is always a little scary, but I know you'll find your place here. Give it a chance."

I nodded, taking a deep breath. Her words wrapped around me like a comforting blanket, easing some of the tension in my chest. With a reluctant sigh, I followed my family into the house. The old house loomed before me, its grand size even more imposing up close. It had weathered, white-painted wood siding and black shutters framing each window. I secretly wondered who puts shutters on houses anymore, although I did like the big patio wrapping around the house. The porch looked inviting with its wooden swing and a few old rocking chairs, creaking softly in the breeze. Above the porch, intricate trim adorned the edges of the roof, giving the house a dollhouse-like charm despite its eerie vibe. The windows were tall and narrow, peering out like eyes, and the front door was a deep, rich red, contrasting sharply with the rest of the house. A couple of large oak trees flanked the house, their branches swaying gently, casting dappled shadows across the lawn.

As my family began unloading boxes and furniture, I couldn't shake the feeling of being watched. I glanced nervously at the neighboring houses, half expecting to see curious eyes peering out from behind curtains. But the streets were empty, save for a few leaves rustling in the breeze. Dad caught my eye as he hoisted a box onto his shoulder, his face uncertain.

"Don't worry, kiddo," he said with a forced grin. "Nothing a little paint can't fix."

"Come on, Addison, don't be such a scaredy-cat," Alex teased, noticing my unease.
"Let's go check out our new rooms!" With a reluctant sigh, I followed my family into the house.

At fourteen, my parents thought I might appreciate having my own space, so they decided the fully finished attic would be perfect for me. The house's interior was spacious and filled with antique furniture, creating a cozy yet slightly eerie atmosphere. As we climbed the narrow staircase to the attic, my anticipation grew. The attic turned out to be large, with slanted ceilings and a row of small windows that let in beams of sunlight.

My eyes widened with wonder as I took in the sight of my new room, already feeling a sense of belonging wash over me. The walls were painted a soft lavender, and the wooden floor had a warm, polished glow. There was even a cozy reading nook by the far window, complete with a plush armchair and a small bookshelf.

"This is amazing!" I exclaimed, a smile spreading across my face for the first time since we had arrived.

"Thank you, Mom and Dad." Mom ruffled my hair, smiling.

"We thought you'd like it. A place all your own to read, study, and just relax."

As I started unpacking, I carefully arranged my books on the small bookshelf and set up my laptop on the desk near the window. The late afternoon sunlight streamed in, casting a warm glow over everything. I felt a sense of accomplishment as I placed my favorite throw blanket over the armchair in the reading nook and organized my school supplies on the desk. Just as I was about to hang up some posters, Mom's voice echoed up the staircase.

"Addison, supper's ready!"

I took a deep breath, catching the delicious scent of pizza wafting up from the kitchen.

My stomach rumbled in response, and I couldn't help but smile. With one last glance around my new room, I headed downstairs, feeling more at home than I had since we'd arrived.

As the sun began to set, casting long shadows across the kitchen floor, 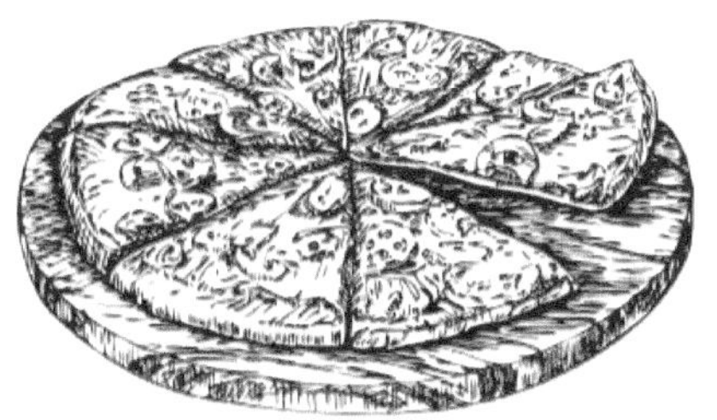 we gathered around a box of pizza in the cozy kitchen. The aroma of cheese and pepperoni filled the room, mixing with the scent of the old wood and faint traces of lavender from the attic.

Despite my earlier apprehension, I found myself feeling excited about the adventures that lay ahead in Salem. Little did I know, our arrival in Salem was just the beginning of a Halloween adventure unlike any other. As the first stars began to twinkle in the twilight sky, a chill ran down my spine.

As we finished our pizza, Dad started telling stories about the town's history, and Alex and I listened intently.

The stories of witches, hauntings, and hidden treasures made my heart race with a mixture of fear and excitement.

"You know," Dad began, his eyes twinkling with mischief, "they say that during the witch trials, there was a woman named Elizabeth.

Proctor who lived not far from here. Legend has it, her spirit still roams the streets of Salem on Halloween night."

Alex's eyes widened. "Do you think we'll see her, Dad?" Mom chuckled, ruffling Alex's hair.

"Don't worry, kiddo. It's just a story." "But what about the hidden treasure?" I asked, leaning forward. "Is there really treasure hidden somewhere in Salem?"

Dad shrugged, a smile playing on his lips. "Who knows? There are many tales of pirates and buried gold around here. Maybe you'll be the one to find it." "Or maybe it's all just old town gossip," Mom interjected with a wink.

"But it's fun to imagine, isn't it?" As the stories continued, my heart raced with a mixture of fear and excitement.

We had moved to Salem for a fresh start, but it seemed we were about to dive into something much deeper and more mysterious than we had ever imagined. Later that night, as I lay in my new attic room, the moonlight cast eerie patterns on the walls. Determination welled up within me, and I silently vowed to uncover whatever mysteries lay ahead. The room, with its cozy reading nook and soft lavender walls, felt like my own private sanctuary, shielding me from the unknowns lurking beyond.

"Goodnight, Addison," I murmured to myself, a strange mix of excitement and anticipation coursing through me. "Welcome to Salem."

My mind buzzed with thoughts of the day ahead—my first day at Salem High. Excitement bubbled up inside me, mingling with a touch of nervousness. I imagined strolling through the halls of the historic school, meeting new friends, and diving into all that Salem had to offer.

✦ Chapter 2 : A Cryptic Encounter ✦

The morning sun filtered through the curtains of my new bedroom, casting a warm glow on the antique

furniture and old-fashioned decor. It was my first day of school in Salem, and I was feeling a mix of excitement and nerves as I got ready for the day ahead. I rummaged through my dresser, searching for my lucky sweater—a soft, worn-out knit that always seemed to bring me comfort in moments of uncertainty. Finding it nestled between stacks of folded clothes, I pulled it on over my favorite jeans.

Downstairs in the kitchen, the aroma of freshly brewed coffee greeted me, mingling with the scent of toast and jam. My parents were already up, sipping on mugs of steaming hot coffee as they discussed their plans for the day.

"Good morning, Addison," Mom greeted me with a smile, her eyes twinkling with excitement.

"Are you ready for your first day at Salem High?" I nodded, trying to muster up some confidence.

"Yeah, I think so. I'm just a bit nervous." Dad chuckled, setting down his coffee mug.

"Don't worry, kiddo. You'll do great. Salem's a town full of history and surprises—you'll fit right in."

With their words of encouragement ringing in my ears, I grabbed a quick breakfast and headed out the door, backpack slung over my shoulder. The walk to school was short but filled with anticipation as I wondered what the day would bring. As I approached the school gates, I couldn't help but feel a sense of awe at the sight before me.

The school was a sprawling brick building with ivy-covered walls and towering oak trees that seemed to whisper secrets in the breeze. It was unlike any school I had ever attended, and I couldn't wait to explore every nook and cranny. Taking a deep breath, I pushed open the heavy wooden doors and stepped inside. The bustling hallways were filled with students chatting and laughing as they made their way to their classes. My heart raced as I navigated the maze of corridors, trying to find my first class of the day. Just as I was about to give up hope of ever finding my way, a voice called out from behind me.

"Hey, are you new here?" I turned to see a girl about my age standing behind me, her curly hair tied back in a messy bun and a mischievous twinkle in her eyes. She wore a black hoodie adorned with patches and pins, giving her a rebellious yet intriguing vibe.

"Yeah, I just moved here yesterday," I replied, relief flooding through me at the sight of a friendly face.

"I'm Addison." The girl grinned warmly, her eyes sparkling with enthusiasm as she gestured towards the big old school with her hands.

"Nice to meet you, Addison. I'm Nova. Welcome to Salem High."

As we chatted, I couldn't help but feel drawn to Nova's easygoing nature and quirky sense of humor. It was as if we had known each other for years rather than just a few minutes. As we walked towards the school, Nova turned to me with a gleam in her eye.

"Hey, do you want to hang out after school?" Her excitement was palpable. "I know this cool spot in the woods where we can explore and maybe even find some spooky stuff."

 I grinned, feeling a surge of excitement. "That sounds awesome! Count me in. "

With Nova by my side and the promise of adventure ahead, I entered Salem High filled with optimism and a growing curiosity about the town's mysteries. Little did I know, meeting Nova was only the start of a friendship that would profoundly shape my life.

The rest of the day went by relatively smoothly. I met a variety of students in my classes, each with their own unique quirks and personalities. One person who stood out was Emma, a blonde girl with glasses who sat next to me in biology. She seemed friendly enough, offering a polite smile and introducing herself when we were assigned to work on a project together. However, when I mentioned that I was meeting up with Nova after school, I noticed a flicker of something in her eyes—an almost imperceptible shift in expression that left me feeling slightly puzzled. Nevertheless, I decided to brush it off, determined to form my own opinions about Nova and our budding friendship.

During lunchtime, as I scanned the bustling cafeteria for a place to sit, I couldn't spot Nova anywhere. I hesitated for a moment, considering joining Emma's table as she waved at me from across the room. After a brief internal debate, I decided to approach Emma's table, curious to get to know her and her friends better.

"Hey, Addison!" Emma greeted me warmly as I joined their table.

"Hey, Emma. Mind if I sit here?" I asked, smiling at her and the other students at the table.

"Of course not! We were just talking about our plans for the weekend," Emma replied, making space for me to sit.

As we chatted and enjoyed our lunch, I found myself enjoying the company of Emma and her friends. They were welcoming and easy to talk to, and I felt a sense of camaraderie as we shared stories and laughed together. After lunch, the afternoon classes passed by in a blur of lectures and note-taking. When the final bell rang, signaling the end of the school day, I felt a mix of anticipation and excitement as I headed to our meeting spot outside the main entrance. As the final bell rang, signaling the end of the school day, I gathered my things and headed outside. To my surprise, there was Nova, waiting for me with a wide grin on her face. It struck me as odd that I hadn't seen her at all during the day.

"Hey, I missed you today at school," I said with a smile.

"You ready for an adventure?" Nova exclaimed excitedly.

Nova avoided the question with a playful wink and simply grabbed my arm, signaling that it was time to go. Without hesitation, we set off on our adventure, leaving the school grounds behind us and venturing into the mysteries of Salem. The anticipation of uncovering secrets and exploring new places filled me with excitement, and I couldn't wait to see where Nova would lead us next.

✦ Chapter 3: The Secret of the Woods ✦

As Nova led me toward the woods, I felt a mix of excitement and fear. The unknown of the woods piqued my curiosity, but honestly, I didn't really know Nova.

I was still thinking about Emma's expression when I mentioned her name—what was that about anyway? The autumn air was crisp and cool, the leaves crunching beneath our feet as we made our way through the dense forest. As we walked, Nova regaled me with tales of Salem's haunted history, her words weaving a tapestry of mystery and intrigue. I listened with rapt attention, captivated by Nova's animated storytelling.

"So, what do you think?" Nova asked, breaking the silence that had settled between us.

"It's amazing," I replied, a sense of wonder filling my voice.
"I never knew Salem was so full of secrets." Nova grinned, her eyes sparkling with excitement.

"Just wait until you see what I have in store for you." Her words gave me pause, and for a moment, I couldn't shake a strange feeling of uncertainty.

How well did I really know Nova? It was a fleeting thought, but it lingered enough to remind me that there was much about this adventurous girl beside me that remained a mystery.

We continued on our journey, winding deeper into the heart of the forest. The trees grew thicker, casting long shadows across the forest floor as the sun began to dip below the horizon.

Finally, we reached a clearing bathed in golden light, the trees parting to reveal a small cabin nestled among the trees. It looked abandoned, its windows boarded up and its roof sagging with age.

"This is it," Nova declared, a triumphant smile spreading across her face. "Welcome to the Witch's Cabin." My eyes widened with awe as I took in the sight before me. The cabin had an eerie aura about it, as if it held secrets long forgotten by time.

"Are you sure it's safe?" I asked, my voice tinged with uncertainty. Nova shrugged, unfazed by my apprehension.

"Only one way to find out." Nova seemed right at home as she confidently opened the door and stepped inside. The interior was dimly lit, the air thick with dust and cobwebs.

With a sense of trepidation, I followed Nova up the creaky wooden steps and into the cabin. Shadows danced along the walls, their movements casting eerie shapes in the flickering candlelight. Suddenly, a floorboard creaked beneath my foot, causing me to jump in surprise. Nova laughed, her voice echoing through the empty room.

"Relax, it's just an old cabin," she reassured me, her eyes twinkling with amusement.

"Nothing to be afraid of." But I couldn't shake the feeling of unease that settled over me like a shroud.

There was something about the cabin that didn't sit right with me, as if it held a darkness that threatened to consume us both. Just as I was about to suggest we leave, Nova's voice broke through the silence.

"Look what I found," she exclaimed, holding up a dusty old book bound in cracked leather.

My eyes widened with curiosity as I peered over Nova's shoulder, the words on the pages illuminated by the flickering candlelight.

"It's a spell book," Nova whispered, her voice filled with awe.

"A real one." As Nova's excitement grew, her eyes sparkled with wonder as she carefully turned the ancient pages of the spell book. My heart raced as I flipped through them, my fingers tracing the faded ink of ancient symbols and incantations. It felt like stumbling upon a forbidden treasure trove of knowledge, offering a glimpse into a world beyond my wildest dreams. Yet, with each passing page, a sense of foreboding crept over me like a tidal wave. The power contained within these pages was palpable, mysterious, and unsettling.

"We shouldn't be here," I whispered, the sound barely escaping my lips over the pounding of my heart.

But Nova was undeterred, her fascination with the spell book evident as she continued to explore its secrets. As shadows deepened around us, a feeling of unease settled in. It was as if we had stirred something dark and dangerous within the Witch's Cabin. As we ventured deeper into the spell book, the air in the cabin grew heavy. The flickering candle flames cast ominous shadows that danced along the walls, heightening the eerie atmosphere.

"This feels wrong," I insisted, my voice tinged with fear. "It's too risky."

But Nova remained absorbed in her study of the ancient runes and incantations, her curiosity overriding any sense of caution.

"Don't be so jumpy, Addison" Nova teased, her voice tinged with impatience. "We're just exploring. What's the harm in that?"

I bit my lip, torn between my desire to be brave and my instincts telling me to flee. I knew we were treading on dangerous ground, but there was a part of me that couldn't resist the allure of the forbidden knowledge that lay before us. Reluctantly, I turned my attention back to the spell book, my fingers tracing the intricate symbols that adorned its pages. Each word seemed to pulse with power, beckoning me closer with a siren's call.

"What does this one say?" I asked, pointing to a particularly cryptic passage written in a language I didn't recognize. Nova leaned in closer, her eyes scanning the ancient text with a furrowed brow.

"It's a summoning spell," she explained, her voice barely above a whisper. "It calls forth shadows from the depths of the underworld."

My heart skipped a beat at Nova's words, a chill running down my spine at the thought of what we were about to unleash. But before I could protest, Nova began reciting the incantation aloud, her voice echoing through the empty cabin like a ghostly whisper.

As the final words fell from Nova's lips, a strange sensation washed over me, as if the very air around us had shifted. The candle flames flickered wildly, casting strange shadows that seemed to dance and twist in the dim light. And then, without warning, the shadows began to merge, swirling together to form a dark, shapeless mass that hovered ominously before us. My breath caught in my throat as I watched in horror, my mind reeling at the sight before me. This was no mere illusion or trick of the light—it was a living, breathing manifestation of the spell we had cast. But before I could react, the shadowy mass surged forward, enveloping us both in its cold, suffocating embrace. I gasped as I felt myself being pulled into the darkness, my mind consumed by fear and uncertainty.

"Nova, what have we done?" I cried, my voice barely audible over the roaring of the shadows.

But Nova was nowhere to be seen, her figure swallowed up by the darkness as it closed in around us. I reached out desperately, my fingers grasping at empty air as I fought to break free from the suffocating grip of the shadows. And then, just as suddenly as it had begun, the darkness receded, leaving me alone in the abandoned cabin, my heart pounding in my chest and my mind reeling from the ordeal.

For a moment, I lay there, panting and disoriented, trying to make sense of what had just happened. But as I glanced around the empty room, my eyes fell upon the spell book lying open on the floor, its pages fluttering in the breeze.

I stood up, feeling the adrenaline still coursing through me, my heart still racing. As I stepped out of the cabin, a shiver ran down my spine. The night air, crisp and cool, did little to shake off the lingering anxiety. The whole ordeal had left me rattled, the shadows and the sudden disappearance of Nova adding layers of unease to an already disorienting situation. Despite the fear that still clung to me, a sense of frustration began to surface. The more I thought about it, the more convinced I became that this was all some elaborate prank. The darkness, the eerie spell book—it all seemed too calculated, too theatrical to be anything other than a carefully staged trick.

As I walked home, the initial dread gave way to irritation. I couldn't shake the feeling that Nova had orchestrated the whole thing to spook me, to watch from the shadows and laugh as I fumbled through her little game. My frustration grew with each step, the lingering fear gradually overshadowed by a resolve to confront her about it. If this was her idea of a joke, she had certainly taken it too far.

By the time I reached the comforting familiarity of my front door, I was still feeling a mix of fear and annoyance. I was eager to return to a semblance of normalcy, to shed the remnants of the unsettling experience and put the pieces together. But the thought of facing Nova and letting her know that her prank had succeeded—perhaps too well—kept gnawing at me as I stepped inside, hoping to find solace in the aroma of Chinese food and the warmth of home.

"Hi, Addison. Where have you been?" she asked, glancing over with a curious smile.

I hesitated, guilt gnawing at me. "Uh, I was at the library. Lost track of time."

Mom raised an eyebrow but smiled understandingly. "That happens when you're engrossed in a good book. Well, dinner's almost ready. Go wash up, dear."

Relieved by her easy acceptance, I nodded and hurried to the bathroom to freshen up. When I returned to the kitchen, Alex was already at the table, chattering excitedly about his day.

"...and then I found this cool bug outside! It had shiny green wings," he exclaimed, his eyes wide with enthusiasm.

Mom chuckled, setting plates of food on the table. "Sounds like quite the discovery, Alex."

Dad entered the kitchen just then, his briefcase in hand.

"Hey there, how was everyone's day?"

"It was great!" Alex replied eagerly, already digging into his food.

I sat down, feeling a mixture of relief and lingering guilt over my half-truth. The warmth of family chatter and the delicious food helped distract me from my unease, at least for the moment. As the night settled in, casting shadows across my room, I lay in bed with a whirlwind of thoughts swirling in my mind. The events of tonight had left me feeling unsettled and uncertain. What was the true nature of the shadowy entity we had summoned? Was it just a figment of our imagination, or had we truly tapped into something beyond our understanding?

Just then, my mom popped her head into my room with her usual comforting smile.

"Hey Addison, just wanted to say goodnight." "Goodnight, Mom. I was just about to turn the lights off," I replied, grateful for her presence.

As she kissed my forehead goodnight and closed the door behind her, I couldn't help but feel a sense of comfort wash over me. Despite the strange occurrences of the evening, I knew that my mom's love and reassurance were constants I could always rely on. However, as I lay there in the darkness, I realized that sleep would not come easily tonight. The events with Nova, the spell book, and the shadowy manifestation kept replaying in my mind like a haunting melody.

I tossed and turned, trying to find a position that would bring me solace, but to no avail. Eventually, I decided to grab my trusty flashlight and the book I had retrieved from the library earlier that day. It was a captivating mystery novel, a welcomed distraction from the unsettling reality I had experienced. I settled back into bed, the warm glow of the flashlight casting a soft light on the pages as I delved into the world of fiction.

As I immersed myself in the story, the hours seemed to slip away. The plot twists and turns captivated my attention, momentarily pulling me away from the uncertainties of the night. It was a temporary escape, but one that provided a much-needed respite from the weight of the evening's events. With each page turn, I felt myself growing drowsy, the fatigue of the day finally catching up to me. Eventually, I set the book aside, turned off the flashlight, and closed my eyes, hoping that sleep would finally claim me. Tomorrow would indeed be a new day—a day filled with questions, conversations, and perhaps even revelations. But for now, I let the soothing rhythm of my breath guide me into the realm of dreams, seeking refuge in the realm where reality and imagination intertwine.

✦ Chapter 4: The Mystery of Nova ✦

The next day at Salem High School, my mind buzzed with unanswered questions as I navigated the crowded hallways.

Nova's sudden disappearance weighed heavily on me, and the eerie feeling that something wasn't right lingered like a shadow at the back of my mind. I couldn't shake off the sense of unease that had settled over me since last night's events.

As I approached my locker, I overheard snippets of conversation from nearby students. Some discussed weekend plans, while others chatted about upcoming assignments. But there was no mention of Nova. It was as if she had vanished into thin air, leaving behind no trace of her existence. Determined to unravel the mystery, I approached a group of classmates gathered by the lockers.

"Hey, have any of you seen Nova?" I asked, trying to keep my tone casual despite the knot of worry tightening in my stomach.

The students exchanged puzzled glances, their brows furrowing in confusion. "Nova who?" one of them replied, shaking their head.

"I don't know anyone by that name." My heart sank.

How could no one at school know Nova? I had been so sure of meeting her, but now it seemed like I had imagined the whole thing.

"She's just a friend," I explained, my voice tinged with disappointment.

"I thought maybe she'd be here today." But the blank stares and shrugs I received in response only deepened the mystery surrounding Nova's disappearance. It was like she had been erased from everyone's memory. Determined to get to the bottom of this, I decided to head to the library during lunch.

The library was a quiet refuge from the bustling hallways, and I hoped it would provide some answers. I made my way to the reference section where the school yearbooks were kept. Pulling out the most recent one, I flipped through the pages, scanning for any sign of Nova. Page after page, I looked at the faces of my classmates, but Nova's face was nowhere to be found. With a growing sense of frustration, I reached the end of the yearbook without any mention of Nova. It was like she had never existed at all. The knot in my stomach tightened as I closed the yearbook and returned it to the shelf. How could this be? Had I really imagined the whole encounter?

But the memories of our conversation, the eerie cabin, and the spell book were so vivid in my mind. As I left the library, I couldn't shake the feeling that something strange was happening in Salem. Determined to find out more, I resolved to keep searching for answers. Nova's disappearance was just the beginning, and I knew I couldn't rest until I uncovered the truth.

But just as I was about to give up hope, a glimmer of inspiration struck. What if Nova wasn't who she appeared to be? What if she was hiding something, something that she didn't want anyone else to know? As I reflected on the events of the day, a particular memory stood out vividly in my mind. It was the look of confusion on Emma's face when I mentioned Nova on my first day at Salem High.

At that time, I had brushed it off, assuming that Emma simply wasn't familiar with Nova because they weren't friends. But now, looking back on it, her expression seemed more than just unfamiliarity; it was genuine confusion. I replayed the scene in my mind, recalling Emma's furrowed brows and slightly puzzled gaze. It was as if she couldn't quite grasp the mention of Nova, as if the name itself held no significance to her. At the time, I hadn't given it much thought, but now, with Nova's sudden disappearance and the mysterious lack of recognition from others, Emma's reaction took on a new meaning.

Perhaps Emma's confusion wasn't about not knowing Nova; maybe it was about the fact that Nova didn't seem to exist in our school's collective memory. The realization sent a shiver down my spine, adding another layer of mystery to the mystery surrounding Nova. Could it be that Nova wasn't just missing but erased from everyone's recollection? The thought was unsettling, to say the least. It raised more questions than answers and added a sense of urgency to my quest for the truth.

The final bell rang, echoing through the corridors of Salem High School, signaling the end of another day.

I gathered my books and slung my backpack over my shoulder, the weight of unanswered questions pressing heavily on my mind. As I stepped out into the cool autumn air, the sun dipped low on the horizon, casting long shadows across the cobblestone streets of Salem.

The town was bathed in the warm glow of the fading daylight, the vibrant colors of fall painting a picture-perfect scene. I walked slowly, lost in thought as I made my way through the bustling streets. The events of the past few days weighed heavily on me, and the mystery of Nova's disappearance loomed large in my mind.

But as I rounded a corner and caught sight of a pumpkin patch nestled on the outskirts of town, a flicker of hope stirred within me. Perhaps the answer to Nova's whereabouts lay hidden among the pumpkins, waiting to be uncovered. With renewed purpose, I made my way towards the pumpkin patch, the scent of cinnamon and spice filling the air as I drew closer. Rows upon rows of pumpkins stretched out before me, their vibrant hues of orange and gold a stark contrast to the fading light of dusk. I wandered among the pumpkins, my fingers tracing the smooth, waxy skin of each one as I searched for any sign of Nova. But try as I might, there was no trace of my elusive friend among the sea of pumpkins.

As the sun sank below the horizon, casting the sky ablaze with hues of pink and orange, I felt a sense of frustration welling up inside me. I had come so close to finding answers, and yet Nova remained as elusive as ever. Just as I was about to give up hope, a voice called out from behind me.

"Addison, is that you?" I turned to see a familiar face approaching through the rows of pumpkins. It was Emma, one of my classmates from school, her eyes wide with curiosity as she caught sight of me.

"Yeah, it's me," I replied, forcing a smile despite the turmoil swirling inside me.

"What are you doing here?" Emma grinned, her cheeks flushed with excitement.

"I come here every year to pick out pumpkins for my family's Halloween decorations. It's a tradition."

My heart skipped a beat at the mention of Halloween. It was just around the corner, and with it came the promise ofspooky stories, costume parties, and the thrill of the unknown. "Hey, do you want to help me pick out a pumpkin?" Emma asked, gesturing towards the rows of pumpkins that stretched out before us.

"It's always more fun with a friend." I hesitated for a moment, torn between my desire to continue searching for Nova and my longing for a sense of normalcy. But then I remembered the warmth of Emma's smile and the promise of Halloween magic, and I knew that I couldn't pass up the opportunity for a bit of fun.

"Sure, I'd love to," I replied, my voice tinged with excitement.

Together, Emma and I spent the evening picking out pumpkins, laughing and chatting as we searched for the perfect ones to adorn our homes. And as we watched the sun set behind the horizon, casting the sky in hues of purple and gold, I couldn't help but feel a sense of hope stirring within me. Perhaps, I thought, there was still magic to be found in Salem after all. And as I looked ahead to the mysteries that lay beyond, I knew that I was ready to face whatever challenges came my way, armed with nothing but my courage and the promise of a new day.

The moon hung low in the sky, casting a silvery glow over the town of Salem as Emma and I walked side by side through the deserted streets. The crisp autumn air sent a shiver down my spine as I clutched my jacket tighter around me, the weight of unanswered questions pressing heavily on my mind. It felt like the night itself held secrets, whispering echoes of the past that begged to be unraveled.

"So, have you found anything out about Nova?" Emma asked, breaking the silence that had settled between us.

I shook my head, my thoughts drifting back to the mysterious disappearance of my mystery friend.

"No, nothing. It's like she never even existed."

Emma frowned, her brow furrowing in confusion. "That's strange. I've never heard of anyone named Nova at our school."

My heart sank at Emma's words. If no one at school knew Nova, then who was she? And why had she disappeared without a trace?

"Actually," Emma continued, her voice tinged with uncertainty, "there is one story I've heard about a girl named Nova." My ears perked up at the mention of Nova's name, a glimmer of hope stirring within me.

"What kind of story?" Emma hesitated for a moment, her gaze fixed on the ground as if searching for the right words.

"It's an old legend, passed down through generations here in Salem. They say there was once a little girl named Nova who lived in these woods. She was said to be a witch, with powers beyond imagining."

My pulse quickened at the mention of witchcraft, my mind racing with possibilities. Could Nova be the same Nova from the legend? And if so, what had happened to her?
"What happened to her?" I asked, my voice barely above a whisper. Emma shrugged, a haunted look in her eyes.

"No one knows for sure. Some say she disappeared into the woods, never to be seen again. Others say she was taken by the darkness that lurks within these woods, consumed by her own powers."

My mind reeled at the thought of Nova being consumed by darkness, my heart heavy with worry. Was it possible that Nova had become trapped in the same darkness we had unleashed in the Witch's Cabin

✦ Chapter 5: Homecoming ✦

My new home stood silent and welcoming as I approached, the soft glow of lamplight spilling out from the windows like a beacon in the gathering dusk. The autumn breeze whispered through the trees, carrying with it the faint scent of wood smoke and fallen leaves. In one hand, I carried a pumpkin that Emma and I had picked out together, and in the other, a cup of warm apple cider. As I stepped through the front door, a sense of warmth and familiarity washed over me, easing the tension that had knotted my shoulders since Nova's disappearance.

"Addison, is that you?" my mother's voice called from the cozy kitchen, the clatter of pots and pans accompanying her words.

"Yeah, Mom, it's me," I replied, my voice tinged with relief as I kicked off my shoes and hung up my coat.

Mom emerged from the kitchen, a warm smile lighting up her face as she caught sight of me. "How was your day, sweetheart?"

"It was...eventful," I admitted, my thoughts drifting back to my encounter with Emma and the unsettling story of Nova.

I held up the pumpkin and the apple cider, smiling. "But I had a great time with Emma. We went to the pumpkin patch and got these." Mom's face softened with a smile.

"That sounds wonderful, Addison. I'm glad you had fun."

Before she could say more, Dad appeared in the doorway, a playful grin spreading across his face.

"Hey there, kiddo! How was your day at school?"
"It was...interesting," I replied, a wry smile quirking my lips as I recounted the day's events. Dad chuckled, ruffling my hair affectionately. "Well, as long as you had fun, that's all that matters."

Just then, my younger brother, Alex, bounded down the stairs with boundless energy, his eyes alight with excitement as he spotted the pumpkin. "

Whoa, cool pumpkin, Addy! Can we carve it together?"

I couldn't help but smile at his enthusiasm. "Sure, Alex. We can carve it together after dinner."

Alex's face lit up with joy as he took the pumpkin out of my hands. "Awesome! I can't wait!"

I watched him dash off towards the kitchen, the pumpkin cradled carefully in his arms. Turning back to my parents, I felt a sense of gratitude wash over me for the loving family that surrounded me, their support a constant source of strength in uncertain times.

"Thanks, Mom, Dad," I said, my voice soft with emotion.

"I'm really glad we moved here." Mom and Dad exchanged a knowing glance, their love for me shining bright in their eyes.

"We're glad too, sweetheart," Mom said, wrapping me in a warm embrace. "Now go on, get settled in. Dinner will be ready soon."

With a final squeeze, I pulled away from Mom's embrace and made my way up to the attic, my footsteps echoing through the silent house. As I reached the top of the stairs, I paused for a moment to take in the sight of my new room, the warm glow of lamplight casting long shadows across the slanted ceiling. Settling into my desk chair, I powered up my computer and opened my browser, my fingers flying across the keyboard as I searched for any mention of Nova or the mysterious legend Emma had told me. But no matter how hard I searched, there was no trace of Nova to be found, her disappearance shrouded in mystery and intrigue.

With a frustrated sigh, I closed my laptop and leaned back in my chair, my mind racing with unanswered questions. But as I gazed out the window at the moonlit sky, a strong sense of purpose welled up within me. I may not have all the answers yet, but I was determined to unravel the mystery of Nova's disappearance, no matter what obstacles lay ahead.

****

As I drifted into sleep, thoughts of Nova lingered on the edges of my consciousness. In my dreams, I found myself standing in the clearing of the forest, surrounded by tall, whispering trees and the lingering scent of damp earth. The moon hung low in the sky, casting eerie shadows that danced around me like specters. And there, standing before me, was Nova. Her dark eyes gleamed with an otherworldly light, her presence both haunting and mesmerizing. She reached out a hand towards me, a silent plea in her gaze. I felt a tug at my heart, a deep sense of connection that defied explanation.

"Nova?" I whispered, my voice lost in the stillness of the forest. But Nova only smiled, a bittersweet expression that spoke volumes. She seemed to shimmer in the moonlight, ethereal and untouchable.

"Find me," her voice echoed in my mind, a faint whisper carried on the wind.

I reached out towards her, my fingers brushing against the cool night air. But just as quickly as she had appeared, Nova began to fade, her form dissipating like mist in the morning sun.

"No, wait!"

I called out, but my words were swallowed by the darkness. And then, with a start, I awoke. The soft glow of lamplight filtered through my window, casting familiar patterns on the walls of my room. My heart raced, my thoughts swirling with the remnants of the dream. Nova's presence lingered in the air, a ghostly whisper that left me yearning for answers.

✦ Chapter 6: In Pursuit of Answers ✦

As I walked to Salem High School, I couldn't shake off the dream I had last night about Nova. The crisp, clear morning air hinted at the onset of winter, but my mind was consumed with thoughts of the mysterious girl who had vanished without a trace. As I approached the school gates, I spotted Emma waiting for me, her curly blonde hair catching the sunlight as she waved enthusiastically.

"Addison, over here!" Emma called, a bright smile lighting up her face as she caught sight of me.

I quickened my pace, a sense of urgency driving me forward as I joined Emma by the gates.

"Hey, Emma," I greeted, my voice tinged with excitement.

"I've been thinking about what you said yesterday, about Nova. Do you think there's any way we could find out more about her?"

Emma furrowed her brow in thought, her eyes scanning the bustling crowds of students heading to class. "Maybe it's worth a shot. We could start asking around, see if anyone knows anything about her."

I nodded eagerly, the prospect of uncovering the truth about Nova filling me with renewed determination. "Yeah, let's do it. Maybe someone here knows something that could help us."

As we made our way through the crowded hallways, we stopped to talk to our classmates, asking if anyone had heard of a girl named

Nova. But each time, we were met with blank stares and shrugs of confusion, leaving us no closer to finding the answers we sought.

"It's like she never even existed," I muttered, frustration bubbling up inside me as we continued our search.

Emma placed a comforting hand on my shoulder, her gaze soft with sympathy. "Don't worry, Addison. We'll find her. We just need to keep looking." With a grateful smile, I nodded, my spirits lifted by Emma's steadfast support. Together, we continued our search, resolved to uncover the truth behind Nova's disappearance, no matter the cost. As the final bell rang, signaling the end of the school day, Emma and I retreated to the library, hoping to find some answers in the pages of dusty old books and forgotten legends.

"I've been doing some research online, but I haven't found anything useful yet," I admitted, my frustration evident in my voice as I scrolled through my failed internet search.

Emma frowned, her gaze fixed on the computer screen as she pondered our next move. "Maybe we're looking in the wrong place. What if Nova's disappearance isn't just a local legend? What if it's part of something bigger, something that goes beyond Salem?"

My eyes widened with realization at Emma's words, a spark of excitement igniting within me. "You mean like a conspiracy or something?" Emma nodded, her expression serious.

"Exactly. What if there's a reason why no one knows anything about Nova? What if someone doesn't want us to find out the truth?"
As the pieces of the puzzle began to fall into place, I felt a sense of clarity wash over me, my mind buzzing with possibilities. Maybe Nova's disappearance wasn't just a coincidence. Maybe there was more to this mystery than meets the eye. But amidst the swirl of theories and possibilities, I couldn't shake off the dream I had last night. Nova's voice echoed in my mind, urging me to find her, to unravel the secrets that shrouded her disappearance. It felt so real, as if

Nova herself was reaching out to me from somewhere beyond.

"Let's keep digging," I said, my voice firm with determination. "We may not have all the answers yet, but I know we're getting close. And when we find out what really happened to Nova, we'll make sure everyone knows the truth."

With a renewed sense of purpose, Emma and I delved deeper into our research, scouring the library for any clues that could lead us to Nova's whereabouts. And as we pored over dusty old tomes and faded newspaper clippings, we knew that we were one step closer to uncovering the truth behind Salem's most haunting mystery.

Little did we know, the answers we sought lay hidden within the shadows of Salem's haunted past, waiting to be discovered by those brave enough to seek them out. And as we embarked on our journey, Emma and I knew that we were ready to face whatever dangers lay ahead, armed with nothing but our courage and the promise of a new day.

✦ Chapter 7: The Secrets Unveiled ✦

As Emma and I sifted through the dusty shelves of the library, I couldn't shake the feeling that we were on the brink of a breakthrough.

The musty scent of ancient paper filled the air, mingling with the excitement and anticipation bubbling inside me. Each book we touched felt like a potential key to unlocking the mystery of Nova's disappearance.

The soft rustle of pages echoed around us, a symphony of forgotten history and hidden secrets. I ran my fingers along the spines of old tomes, my heart racing with each discovery, no matter how small. Every turn of a page brought us closer to the truth we were so desperately seeking.

"This one looks promising," Emma remarked, pulling out a weathered book with a faded title that hinted at arcane knowledge.

I leaned in closer, my eyes scanning the yellowed pages as if they held the answers we sought.

"Let's see what it says." As we delved into the text, I felt a surge of excitement.

The book contained references to ancient rituals, mystical symbols, and hidden societies. It was like stepping into a world of magic and mystery, a world that seemed far removed from our own but held tantalizing clues about Nova's mysterious past.

"This could be it," I whispered, my voice filled with hope and determination. "We might finally be getting somewhere."

Emma nodded, her eyes alight with curiosity as she read alongside me. Together, we pieced together fragments of information, connecting dots that seemed unrelated at first but formed a compelling narrative. The more we read, the more convinced I became that Nova's disappearance was tied to something much bigger than we had initially imagined. Hours passed in a blur as we lost ourselves in the pages of forgotten lore. The sun dipped lower in the sky, casting long shadows across the library, but we didn't notice. We were consumed by our search, driven by a relentless need to uncover the truth. And then, just as we were about to give up hope, Emma let out a gasp.

"Addison, look at this!" I turned to see what had caught her attention, my heart pounding with anticipation.

Emma pointed to a passage in the book, a passage that spoke of a secret society known as the Keepers of the Shadows. According to the text, this society was rumored to possess ancient knowledge and wielded powers beyond mortal comprehension.

"This is it," I breathed, my eyes wide with realization. "The Keepers of the Shadows. They must be connected to Nova somehow."

Excitement and trepidation mingled in my chest as we delved deeper into the secrets of the Keepers. Each revelation brought us closer to understanding Nova's role in this hidden world, but it also raised new questions and uncertainties.

As the library grew dimmer with the fading light, Emma and I exchanged determined looks. We knew that our journey was far from over. The trail of clues we had uncovered was leading us down a path fraught with danger and intrigue, but we were ready to follow it to the end, no matter where it led us. As I stared at the black-and-white photograph, a mix of awe and confusion swept over me. Here was Nova, standing defiantly in a circle of women whose identities were shrouded by shadows and time. The date on the back, 1692, linked this mysterious image to the infamous Salem witch trials. Questions flooded my mind like a torrential downpour, each one vying for attention.

"What does this mean?" I whispered, my voice barely escaping my lips as I traced the faces in the photograph.

Emma, equally captivated by the discovery, leaned in closer to examine the details.

"It's like she was part of something... bigger," Emma mused, her eyes scanning the faded features of the women. "But why would Nova be connected to the Salem trials? And how does this tie into her disappearance?"

I shook my head, the weight of unanswered questions pressing down on me.

"I don't know, Emma. But this feels significant. We need to find out more about these women, especially Elizabeth Proctor."

As we delved deeper into our research, the library transformed into a focal point of secrets and whispers from centuries past. We poured over historical records, newspaper clippings, and obscure texts, piecing together a story that defied logic and reason. Elizabeth Proctor's name surfaced repeatedly, intertwined with accusations of witchcraft and the hysteria that gripped Salem.

"But why is Nova connected to Elizabeth Proctor?" I pondered aloud, my voice echoing in the silent library. "And what does this have to do with her disappearance?"

Emma's eyes narrowed as she read through an article about Elizabeth Proctor's trial. "There's something here, Addison.

Something about a hidden coven and a pact made in shadows.

"My heart raced at the mention of a hidden coven, the pieces of the puzzle beginning to align in my mind.

"What if Nova was part of this coven? What if she knew something that others wanted to keep hidden?"

The thought sent a shiver down my spine, the weight of conspiracy and danger hanging heavy in the air. But alongside the fear was a burning curiosity, a resolve to unearth the truth no matter how deep it was buried.

"We have to keep digging," I declared, my voice firm with resolve. "There's more to Nova's story than meets the eye, and we won't stop until we uncover the whole truth."

With newfound resolve, Emma and I continued our quest for answers. The library, once a quiet sanctuary of knowledge, became a battleground of secrets and revelations. And as we pieced together the threads of Nova's past, I knew that we were on the brink of uncovering a truth that would shake Salem to its core.

✦ Chapter 8: Echoes of the Past ✦

In the dim light of an old Salem cottage, a mother and her two daughters huddled together, their faces drawn with fear as the shadows of persecution loomed outside. The year was 1692, and the witch trials had cast a dark cloud over the town, claiming innocent lives in the name of fear and superstition. Elizabeth Proctor, the elder daughter, held her mother's hand tightly, her eyes filled with steadfast determination as she vowed to protect her family at all costs. Nova, the younger daughter, clung to her sister's side, her heart pounding with terror as she watched the flames of hysteria engulf their once peaceful town. But as the accusations grew louder and the noose tightened around their necks, the Proctor family found themselves torn apart by forces beyond their control. Their mother, a healer and wise woman accused of witchcraft, was dragged away in chains, leaving behind nothing but a trail of sorrow and despair. Desperate to save their mother, Elizabeth and Nova turned to the only power they had left—magic. Together, they embarked on a dangerous journey to summon their mother's spirit and bind her to their side, hoping to protect her from the horrors of the trial. But as the incantations echoed through the night and the candles flickered in the darkness, disaster struck. A surge of power overwhelmed them, tearing Nova away from her family and casting her into the depths of the unknown. For centuries, Nova wandered the shadows, her heart filled with longing for the family she had lost. She searched tirelessly for her mother and sister, her memories fragmented and her soul adrift in a sea of darkness. And as the years passed and the world changed around her, Nova clung to the hope that one day, she would be reunited with her loved ones and find the peace she so desperately sought. But little did she know, the echoes of the past were about to resurface, and the secrets that had long been buried would be brought to light once more. And as Nova's path collided with the present, she would come face to face with the truth about her family and the role she was destined to play in the fate of Salem.

✦ Chapter 9: Shadows of the Harvest Moon ✦

The night air was alive with excitement as Emma and I made our way through the streets of Salem, the sounds of laughter and music drifting on the cool autumn breeze. The town was  brimming with the spirit of Halloween, its streets adorned with jack-o'-lanterns and decorations that glowed in the light of the full moon.

"It's amazing how everyone comes together to celebrate Halloween in Salem," Emma remarked, her eyes sparkling with excitement as she took in the sights and sounds around us. I nodded in agreement, my heart pounding

with anticipation for the night ahead. "Yeah, it's like the whole town comes alive with magic."
As we wandered through the crowded streets, I couldn't shake the feeling that we were being watched. The hairs on the back of my neck stood on end as I scanned the shadows for any sign of danger, but all I saw were smiling faces and the flickering glow of jack-o'-lanterns.

"Do you ever get that feeling?" I asked Emma, my voice low.

"What feeling?" she replied, her eyes darting around.

"Like someone's watching you," I said, trying to sound casual but failing miserably.

Emma chuckled softly, shaking her head. "It's probably just your imagination," she reassured me, her voice tinged with amusement.

"You're not scared, are you?" I forced a smile, trying to push aside my unease.

 "Of course not," I lied. "It's just... everything feels so intense tonight." Emma nodded, her expression turning thoughtful.
"Yeah, I get what you mean. There's definitely something in the air. Maybe it's just the Halloween vibes."

"Maybe," I said, though I wasn't convinced.

Emma nudged me playfully. "Come on, lighten up. Look at all these people having fun. We're here to enjoy ourselves too, remember?"

I glanced around at the revelers, their laughter and joy infectious.

"You're right," I admitted, trying to relax. "Let's make the most of it."

"That's the spirit!" Emma exclaimed, linking her arm with mine. "Let's go find the spookiest haunted house. I heard there's one with a real ghost story behind it." I laughed, feeling some of the tension leave my body.

"Alright, lead the way."

As we reached the outskirts of town, the streets grew quiet, and the sounds of revelry faded into the distance.

The moon hung low in the sky, casting an eerie glow over the deserted streets as we made our way toward the house where Nova had disappeared.

"I can't believe we're actually going to see the house where Nova vanished," Emma exclaimed, her eyes wide with excitement.

"Do you think we'll find any clues about what happened to her?" I shrugged, my thoughts consumed by the mystery that had been haunting me for weeks.

"I don't know, but I have a feeling we're about to find out."

"Remember how we heard those rumors about the house being haunted?" Emma said, her voice barely above a whisper.

"I thought it was just Halloween tales, but now..." "But now it feels real," I finished for her, my heart pounding.

As we approached the house, our breath caught in our throats at the sight before us. The windows were ablaze with light, and the sound of chanting filled the air as shadows danced across the walls.
"What the hell is going on in there?" Emma whispered, her eyes wide with fear and curiosity.

"I don't know," I replied, my voice shaking. "But we need to find out."

As we approached the house, our breath caught in our throats at the sight before us.

The windows were ablaze with light, and the sound of chanting filled the air as shadows danced across the walls.

"What's going on?" Emma whispered, her voice barely audible over the roar of the crowd. I shook my head, my heart racing with fear and anticipation as we crept closer to the house.
"I don't know, but we need to be careful."

We ducked behind a bush, our hearts pounding in our chests as we watched in horror. Nova appeared in the window, her hands raised in a strange and ancient gesture as she chanted incantations that sent shivers down our spines. But as we watched, our blood ran cold at the sight of figures emerging from the shadows— the ghosts of the people who had brought down Nova's mother all those years ago.

Their faces twisted with hatred and malice as they hurled curses and spells at Nova, their voices echoing through the night like the wails of the damned.

"We have to do something," Emma whispered, her eyes wide with fear as she watched the battle unfold before us. I nodded, my mind racing with fear and uncertainty as we made our way to the window of the house.

The air crackled with magic as we peered inside, our hearts pounding in our chests as we watched Nova and the ghosts locked in a fierce battle for control. But just as it seemed like all hope was lost, Nova's eyes met ours, her expression filled with determination and courage as she continued to fight against the forces of darkness.

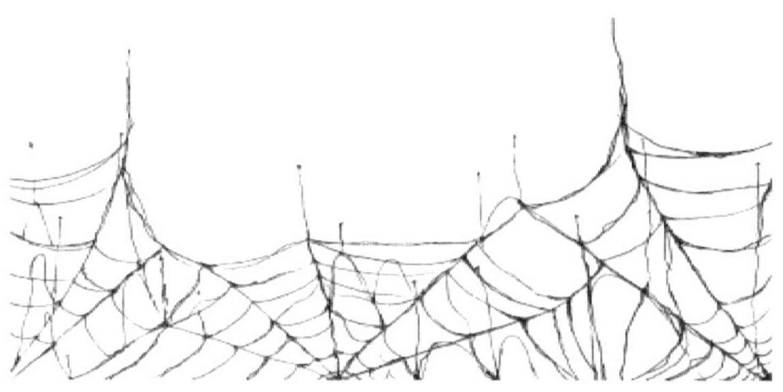

"We have to help her," I declared, my voice tinged with urgency as we leaped through the window and joined the fray.

As Nova's eyes met ours, a surge of courage filled her heart. With a final burst of energy, she channeled all her magic into the last part of the spell. The air crackled with power as Emma and I watched in awe. Suddenly, as Nova completed the incantation, the house was engulfed in darkness. A deafening silence fell over the night, broken only by the sharp intake of breath from Emma and me. Then, unable to contain our fear and exhilaration any longer, we let out a simultaneous scream that echoed through the night, our voices mingling with the fading echoes of the spell. As Emma and I prepared to bolt from the darkness enveloping the house, my gaze caught a low glow amidst the shadows. It flickered like a distant ember, casting an ethereal light that seemed to beckon us closer. Strangely, it bore a resemblance to Nova, yet somehow different—more like the girl in the picture we had found. As we continued to stare in disbelief, the glow intensified, revealing two other figures standing alongside it. They bore a striking resemblance to Elizabeth and her mother, their features etched with determination and a hint of sadness. A shiver ran down my spine as I realized the significance of what we were witnessing—echoes of the past, reaching out from the depths of history to intertwine with the present. Nova, Elizabeth, and their mother stood before us, their forms glowing with a soft, otherworldly light. The ancient magic that had torn them apart centuries ago now seemed to bind them together, their spirits connected across time and space. Emma and I watched in awe as the spectral figures moved closer, their eyes filled with a mixture of sorrow and hope.

"Thank you," Nova whispered, her voice barely audible over the crackling energy that surrounded us.

"You have given us a chance to be together again."

As the figures began to fade, I felt a surge of warmth and gratitude wash over me. The echoes of the past had finally found peace, their stories woven into the fabric of Salem's history.

Emma and I stood in silence, the weight of the moment settling over us as we realized the enormity of what we had witnessed.

"She did it" Emma said softly, her voice filled with wonder.

"She actually did it." I nodded, a sense of fulfillment and resolve filling my heart.

"Yes, she did. And now, we have to make sure their story is never forgotten." With that, we turned away from the house, our steps light with the knowledge that we had played a part in reuniting a family torn apart by history. As we walked back through the streets of Salem, the town seemed to shimmer with a newfound magic, the spirit of Halloween forever intertwined with the echoes of the past.

And as the Harvest Moon cast its gentle glow over Salem, I knew that our journey was far from over. The shadows of the past had been illuminated, but new mysteries awaited us in the days to come. Together, Emma and I were ready to face whatever challenges lay ahead, united by the courage and determination that had brought us this far.

✦ Chapter 10: A Time for Gratitude ✦

As Thanksgiving approached, my family had settled comfortably into our new life in Salem. The crisp autumn air

carried the scent of pumpkin spice and fallen leaves, and the streets were alive with the hustle and bustle of holiday preparations. I awoke to the soft glow of dawn filtering through my window, a sense of warmth and contentment filling my heart. Stretching lazily, I relished the comfort of my cozy attic room before making my way downstairs to join my family for breakfast.

The kitchen was alive with the sound of sizzling bacon and bubbling coffee as my parents bustled about, preparing a hearty meal to start the day.

My younger brother, Alex, sat at the table, eagerly digging into a stack of pancakes as he regaled our parents with tales of his latest adventures.

"Good morning, sleepyhead," Mom greeted me with a smile as I entered the room. "Did you sleep well?" I nodded, a smile spreading across my face as I took my seat at the table.

"Yeah, I feel great. It's hard to believe Thanksgiving is just around the corner."

"I know, right?" Alex chimed in, his mouth full of pancake. "I can't wait for the turkey and all the pie!"

 Dad chuckled, setting a plate of steaming pancakes in front of me. "Time flies when you're having fun, huh? Have you thought about what you're thankful for this year, Addison?"

I paused, considering. "Honestly, I'm just thankful for how well we've settled into Salem. I wasn't sure about moving here at first, but now it feels like home."

 Mom smiled warmly. "I'm thankful for that too. And I'm grateful for all the new friends we've made here. It's really starting to feel like we're part of the community."
"And don't forget the big Thanksgiving parade," Alex added excitedly.

"I heard it's going to be amazing this year!"

 "That's right," Dad said, pouring himself a cup of coffee. "We should all go together. It'll be a great way to kick off the holiday season."

After breakfast, I made my way to school, my heart light with anticipation for the day ahead. The streets were alive with the chatter of students making their way to class, their laughter mingling with the rustle of fallen leaves underfoot. As I entered the school building, I was greeted by the familiar sight of my friends gathered in the courtyard, their faces alight with excitement as they chatted and laughed together. I joined them with a smile, feeling grateful for the sense of belonging they had brought into my life.

"Hey, Addison!" Emma called out, waving me over.

"We were just talking about our plans for the slumber party. Are you excited?"

"Absolutely," I replied, my grin widening. "I've got some spooky stories lined up for us."

The morning passed in a blur of classes and laughter, and before I knew it, the lunch bell rang, signaling the start of the afternoon session. My friends and I made our way to the cafeteria, our voices echoing off the walls as we discussed our plans for the upcoming holiday. We eagerly shared ideas for the slumber party, our excitement building with each passing moment. It was moments like these, surrounded by friends who felt like family, that I cherished the most. As the bell rang, signaling the start of our next class, Emma and I made our way to our seats, chatting animatedly about our plans for the upcoming slumber party.

"I was thinking we could make it a costume theme," Emma suggested. "What do you think?"

 "That's a great idea!" I said, already imagining the fun we'd have. "Maybe we can even have a mini Halloween in November."

We settled into our desks, our excitement palpable in the air around us. But as we exchanged glances, our conversation halted abruptly as the teacher entered the room, drawing our attention to the front.

"Good morning, class," the teacher began, her voice commanding attention. "I have an announcement to make. We have a new student joining us today."

Emma and I exchanged puzzled looks, our curiosity piqued. As the door opened once again, our eyes widened in disbelief as a familiar figure stepped into the room. It was a girl who bore a striking resemblance to Nova.

Confusion and surprise painted our expressions as we exchanged glances once more, our minds racing with questions. How could this be possible? Was it really Nova? Or was it just a coincidence? Our shared sense of unease and bewilderment lingered as the teacher continued with the class, leaving Emma and me to ponder the mysterious arrival of the new student.

Acknowledgements

I would like to extend my heartfelt thanks to the GG Group. Your invaluable input and diligent reading of all my edits have been crucial in shaping this book. I deeply appreciate your support and dedication throughout this long process.

A special thank you to Melinda, whose constant support and keen eye have been invaluable. Your dedication in reading and rereading this book has made all the difference. Thank you for being a constant source of encouragement and for believing in this story as much as I do.

To Rebecca, thank you for listening to all my crazy ideas and encouraging me to pursue them. Your belief in my creativity has been a source of inspiration.

To my husband, your unwavering support and love have been my foundation. Without you, none of this would be possible. You are my rock, and I am forever grateful for your presence in my life.

Thank you all for being part of this journey.

* 9 7 8 1 0 6 9 0 0 0 2 0 0 *